1922

Alex and the Cat

by **Helen V. Griffith**

pictures by **Joseph Low**

Greenwillow Books, New York

Library of Congress Cataloging in Publication Data
Griffith, Helen V.   Alex and the cat.
(A Greenwillow read-alone book)
Summary: Three stories about Alex , who
wants to be treated like the family cat,
or live wild like a wolf, and who tries
to restore a baby bird to a robin's nest.
[1. Dogs–Fiction.   2. Animals–Fiction]
I. Low, Joseph, (date),   ill.   II. Title.
III. Series: Greenwillow read-alone books.
PZ7.G8823 A1   [E]   81-11608
ISBN 0-688-00420-2   AACR2
ISBN 0-688-00421-0 (lib. bdg.)

1922

FOR NATALIE

-H.V.G.

FOR BINKY

-J.L.

Contents

Alex the Cat

"I wish I were a cat,"
said Alex.

The cat was curled up
with his eyes shut.
"Um," he said.
"Cats can do just as they please,"
said Alex.
The cat opened his eyes.
"Since when?" he asked.

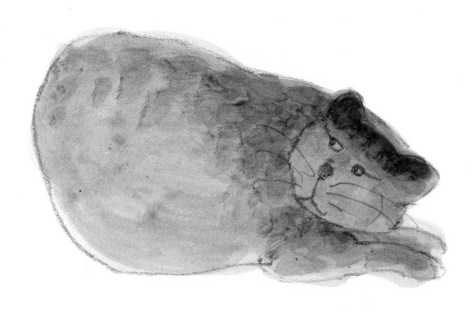

"Cats can stay out
   all night," said Alex.
"That's true," said the cat.
"Nobody gives them baths,"
   said Alex.
"Certainly not," said the cat.
"And they don't do tricks,"
   said Alex.
"You've made your point,"
   said the cat.

"Who wants a snack?"
called Robbie.

Alex and the cat
ran to the kitchen.

"Hi, kitty.

Sit, Alex,"

said Robbie.

See that? Alex said

to himself.

He sat and wished he were a cat

until Robbie said,

"Do your tricks, Alex."

Alex knew two tricks.

He did them both.

"Good Alex," said Robbie.

He gave Alex a biscuit.

Then Robbie poured the cat

some milk.

See that? Alex said to himself.

He sat and wished he were a cat

until Robbie said,

"Lesson time, Alex."

Robbie and Alex and the cat

all ran outside.

Robbie was teaching Alex

to sit up.

Alex could not get it right.

Sometimes he fell over backwards.

Sometimes he fell over sidewards.

But he kept trying.

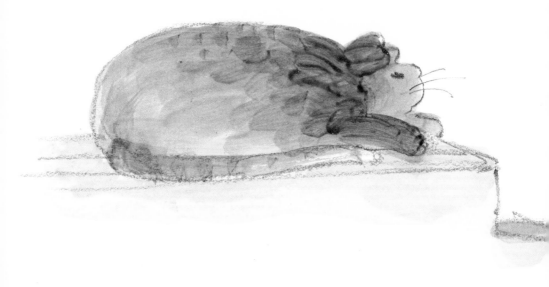

Then he saw the cat

sitting on the step doing nothing.

See that? Alex said to himself.

He lay down with his chin

on his paws.

"Alex, what's wrong?"

asked Robbie.

Alex didn't move.

"Are you sick?"
asked Robbie.
Alex still didn't move.
"Rest awhile, Alex,"
Robbie said,
and he went
into the house.

The cat walked over to Alex.

"What's the matter?" he asked.

"Nothing," said Alex.

"I'm just being a cat."

"You can't be a cat," said the cat.

"I can act like one," said Alex.

He lay very still

with his chin on his paws.

The cat lay down beside him
and purred to himself.
After a while
Alex raised his head.
"This is boring," he said.
"Not to me," said the cat.

Alex sighed
and put his chin
back on his paws.
"I'll never learn
to sit up now," he said.
"Cats don't sit up anyway,"
said the cat.
Robbie came outside.
Alex was so glad to see him
that he forgot to be a cat.
He sat up and waved his paws.
He swayed a little,
but he didn't fall.

"Alex!" shouted Robbie.

"You're sitting up!"

I really am! thought Alex.

He fell over backwards

from excitement,

but he sat up again right away.

It was easier this time.

Now I know three tricks,

he thought.

He did them all,

one after another.

Then he sat down
beside the cat to rest.
Being a dog is not easy,
Alex said to himself,
but it's interesting.

Alex
Leaves Home

Alex was tired
of being a pet.
"I want to live in the wilderness
like the wolves," he told the cat.
"You're kidding," said the cat.

"I'll go out tonight
when you do," said Alex.
The cat rubbed his ear
and yawned.
"Then I'll join the wolves
and be a wild animal,"
said Alex.

The cat closed his eyes
and purred to himself.
"Are you listening?"
asked Alex.
"I'm listening," said the cat
between purrs,
"in my own way."

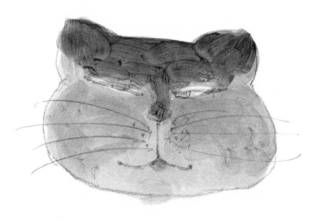

That night
Alex and the cat
left the house together.
The cat led Alex
down the steps
and across the yard
and over the fence.

"Is this the wilderness?"
asked Alex.

"As far as I know," said the cat.

"Where are the wolves?"

asked Alex.

"I've never seen any," said the cat,

"but then, I've never looked."

"Is it always this cold?"

asked Alex.

"Sometimes it's colder," said the cat,

crouching in the grass.

"What do you do out here

all night?" asked Alex.

"I have my interests," said the cat.

"Excuse me."

He leaped into the darkness.

Alex stood shivering
until he came back.
"Did I hear a squeak?"
asked Alex.
"Probably," said the cat,
washing his face with his paw.

Alex looked and listened

and sniffed the air.

"I can't find any wolves," he said.

"Find a rabbit," said the cat.

"What for?" asked Alex.

The cat looked at him.

"To eat," he said.

"Oh," said Alex,

"I couldn't eat a rabbit."

"Wolves eat rabbits," said the cat.

"Oh," said Alex.

A huge shadow swept over them.
Alex yelped and
threw himself on the ground.

The cat snarled

and clawed the air.

The shadow flew away.

"What was it?" asked Alex.

"An owl," said the cat.

"Could it hurt us?"
asked Alex.

"Probably," said the cat.

"Weren't you afraid?"
asked Alex.

The cat shook his fur into place
and smoothed his whiskers.
"I was afraid," he said,
"in my own way."

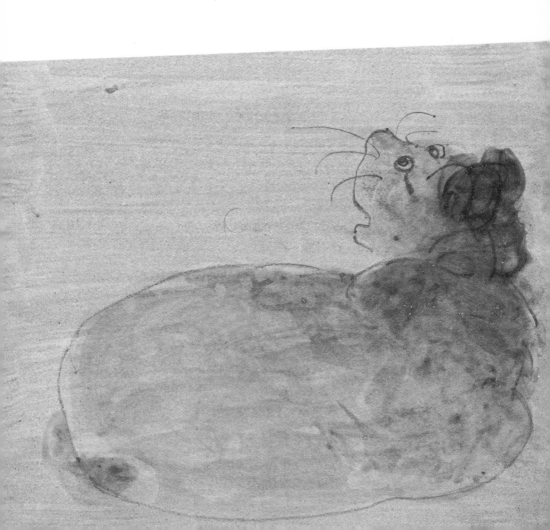

It began to rain.

"Oh, no," said Alex.

"What do you do when it rains?"

"I sleep in a basket
   on the porch," said the cat.

"It's very snug."

"What do wolves do?"
   asked Alex.

"I wouldn't know," said the cat,
 turning toward the fence.

"Good night."

"I've been thinking," said Alex.

"Have you?" asked the cat, waiting.

"Robbie will miss me," said Alex.

"Probably," said the cat.

"I think I'll go home," said Alex.

"Suit yourself," said the cat,
   and he jumped over the fence.
   Alex jumped after him.
"Is there room for me
   in the basket?" he asked.
"I doubt it," said the cat.

"Then I'll scratch
on the door," said Alex.
Alex and the cat ran
across the yard and up the steps
and onto the porch.
Alex scratched on the door
and sat down to wait.

"Robbie would be surprised
at my adventures," he said.
The cat brushed the raindrops
from his fur and
jumped into his basket.
"To him I'm just a pet,"
said Alex.
The cat made his eyes into slits
and began to purr softly.
"Just think," said Alex,
"I almost ran away
with the wolves."

The cat snuggled down
in the basket
and closed his eyes.
"You almost did," he purred,
"in your own way."

Alex's Peaceful Day

Alex was lying in the grass
thinking of nothing.

In the yard next door
chickens were clucking.
In their nest in the rosebush
robins were cheeping.
It was a peaceful day.
Alex closed his eyes.

PEEP! PEEP!

Alex opened his eyes.

A little bird was standing there.

"PEEP! PEEP!" it said.

It sat on the grass

and looked at Alex.

"Are you lost?" asked Alex.

"PEEP! PEEP!" said the little bird.

"You must have fallen out
of your nest," said Alex.

Just then a robin

with a worm in her beak

flew into the rosebush.

"There is your mother now,"
said Alex.
He ran over to the rosebush.
"Here is one of your babies,"
he called.
"All of my babies are
in their nest," said the robin,
and she flew away.
She can't count, thought Alex.
She doesn't know a baby is missing.

He looked at the little bird.

It was pecking at insects in the grass.

The insects were getting away.

"The bird is hungry," said Alex.

"It needs its mother."

Alex sat on the grass

and thought.

It's up to me

to help this bird,

he decided.

"Don't be afraid,"
he told the baby bird,
and he picked it up in his mouth.
"PEEP! PEEP!" shouted the bird.
Alex held it very carefully
and carried it to the rosebush.
I hope I don't
swallow this bird, he thought.

The bird flapped its wings
and kicked its legs.
I hope I don't sneeze
and swallow this bird,
thought Alex.

He pushed his nose
into the rosebush.
He opened his mouth
and the little bird
dropped into the nest.
"I did it," said Alex.

The robin flew to her nest again.

She had a moth in her beak.

"I wonder if she will notice

that her baby is back,"

Alex said.

The robin dropped the moth.

"EEEEK!" she screamed.

"She noticed," said Alex.

"Who put this chicken in my nest?"
screamed the robin.
"You mean that is not your baby?"
asked Alex.
"It is a chicken," said the robin,
"and it can't stay here."
"Oh my," said Alex.
He pushed his nose
back into the rosebush.
He took the baby chick
in his mouth.
Thorns were scratching him.

The robin was flying
around his head and screaming.
The chick was kicking and flapping.

I am going to swallow this bird yet,
thought Alex.

He backed out of the rosebush
with the chick in his mouth,
just as a big red chicken
came through the fence.

"PEEP! PEEP!" called the baby chick.

"AWWWWK!" called the hen.

She started toward Alex.

Alex dropped the baby chick.

"I can explain," he said.

The hen fluffed out her feathers.

She spread her wings wide.

"AWWWWK!" she said again.

"Oh my," said Alex.
Just then the cat came
from somewhere.
He sat beside Alex
and yawned.
The hen stood still.
She looked at Alex
and the cat
sitting side by side.

"Awk," she said.
She shook her feathers
back into place.
She clucked to her baby
and went back
through the fence.

The little chick

looked at Alex.

"Peep, peep," it said.

Then it ran after its mother.

Alex turned to the cat.

"She thought I was going to

hurt her baby," he said.

"I know," said the cat.

"I wasn't though," said Alex.

He told the cat

the whole story.

The cat blinked his eyes
at Alex.
"You mean you can't tell a robin
from a chicken?" he asked.
"I can now," said Alex.

Alex and the cat lay
side by side on the warm grass.
Chickens were clucking.
Robins were cheeping.
The cat was purring.
Alex closed his eyes
and thought of nothing.
It was a peaceful day.

HELEN V. GRIFFITH grew up in Wilmington, Delaware, where she still lives. She works in her family's roofing and siding business, and on books for young readers in her spare time. She is an ardent bird-watcher and spends her vacations adding new species to her list. Her first book, *Mine Will, Said John*, is also about a puppy.

JOSEPH LOW was born in Pennsylvania, grew up in Illinois, studied art in New York City, and taught at Indiana University for several years. His prints and private press publications have been widely shown and collected by museums and libraries. He is the illustrator of more than forty books for children, and the author-artist of *Mice Twice* (a Caldecott Honor Book) and *Benny Rabbit and the Owl*, among others. He lives in Martha's Vineyard during the summer and the Caribbean during the winter.